The illustrations in this book are hand-drawn using gouache and pen.

Translated by Polly Lawson
First published in Dutch as *Kersenhemel* by Em Querido's
Uitgeverij in 2017
First published in English by Floris Books in 2019
First published in the USA in 2020

British Library CIP Data available
ISBN 978-178250-561-7
Printed in China through Imago

Cherry Blossom and Paper Planes

Jef Aerts & Sanne te Loo

Floris Books

Some friends are more than friends.
They grow like twin cherries
    from the same stem.

Just like Dina and Adin,
who knew what the other one was thinking,
    even without talking.

Adin and Dina lived on a farm.
Dina lived at the top of the hill.
Adin lived at the bottom of the hill.
Adin's mother worked on the farm picking fruit.

The hillsides were covered with fruit trees:
    peaches and plums,
        apricots and cherries.
Especially cherries.
Sweet black fruit, sour red fruit,
and yellow fruit with a shy pink blush.

Dina and Adin liked to help on the farm.
For every cherry they picked, they ate one too.
They drew on each other's cheeks with cherry juice.

Adin was as agile as a cat.

He swung gracefully from branch to branch.

Dina climbed carefully, with a bag in each hand.

One for the cherries, one for the pits.

Dina and Adin's special game was planting
    cherry pits in the village.
In cracks and crevices,
    between paving stones,
    on the green beside the café,
    and the road outside the bakery.

"The juiciest cherries will grow here one day," said Dina, smiling.
And when Dina smiled, Adin's eyes smiled with her.

One afternoon, Dina and Adin lay on the grass
looking up at the cherry-tree sky.
"Mama wants a different job," said Adin,
"in the city."
Dina held her breath, then asked,
"Couldn't she do a different job here?"
Adin said, "We're moving next week."

"Will you ever come back?" asked Dina.
"Mama says leaving is like coming back," sighed Adin,
"just the other way round."
Dina shrugged her shoulders.
"I hate the other way round."

A week went by.
Dina and Adin sat in a cherry tree,
   back to back.
"Come down, Adin!" his mother called.
   "It's time to go."
Dina gave Adin her bag of cherry pits.
"Self-picked and self-spat out," she said.

Corey, Adin's pet crow, hopped from his hand
    onto Dina's shoulder.
"Give him your leftovers," Adin said,
    "and he'll follow you everywhere."
Dina waved goodbye
    as her friend disappeared into the distance.

Dina's summer felt long and lonely
    without Adin to play with.

Corey slept outside Dina's bedroom,
    on the windowsill.
He cawed happily when she woke up,
    and flew alongside her when she cycled to school.
But even that didn't make Dina feel better.

Adin felt lonely too.

From the balcony of his tenth-floor apartment,
   he threw Dina's cherry pits
    as far as he could above the city.
He watched them soar, then fall,
   but they never flew further than the fountain across the road.

He wished they could fly
           all the way back to the farm.
                    All the way back to Dina.

Before long it started to get colder,
    and Dina's father took her to the city to buy a new coat.
"Perhaps we can visit Adin while we're there," he said.
Dina smiled.

It took a long time to find Adin's building.
Dina looked carefully for the right bell to ring.

They went up in an elevator to the tenth floor.
Adin was waiting outside on the balcony,
    wearing smart clothes,
    with his hair neatly combed.
He looked different from the Adin Dina knew,
    the boy with cherry-juice cheeks.
"Hi," he said.
"Hi," Dina said back.
For a moment, they forgot everything
    they had been waiting so long to tell each other.

Then Adin said, "Watch this!"
He folded a sheet of paper into a plane
  and wedged a few cherry pits between the wings.
He threw the plane into the air.

It floated high above the rooftops,
  swooping up and down on the breeze.
The pits fell like autumn leaves around the city.
Dina and Adin turned to each other and smiled.

Weeks passed,
  and the wind blew icy-cold on the hillsides.
Dina sat under the bare cherry trees.
She hugged her new coat tightly around her
  and thought of Adin, far away in the city.
Then she got on her bicycle...

...and cycled away from the quiet farmhouse,
away from the empty caravan,
towards Adin.

And along the way,
she pushed cherry pits into the frozen ground
until her bag was empty.
Then she cycled back home.

All winter long, high up in his apartment,
   Adin folded paper gliders,
   jumbo jets and stunt planes.

When the wind was right, he launched them
   away from the fountain across the road,
   away from the busy shopping streets,
      towards Dina.

And along the way,
         the pits drilled little holes in the snow,
                    like tiny footprints.

At long last, the smell of spring arrived,
    fresh and green.
Dina filled her lungs with it.
Corey swooped and glided happily
    between cobweb clouds.

Dina climbed to the top of a cherry tree,
    much higher than she usually dared,
    until she could see the city's smoke rising
    in the soft spring sky.

Adin breathed the spring air too,
    as the city's rooftops glimmered in the sunshine.
He had only one pit left now.
Tucking it into a paper plane,
    he threw it towards the faraway hills.

And as Dina looked towards Adin,
    and Adin looked towards Dina,
    a spark of true friendship flew between them,
    even though they were far apart,
        and …

…the cherry trees started to bloom.

Buds swelled until they burst into blossom.
A carpet of flowers rolled out over the land,
	from Dina's orchards,
	past villages and farms,
	to the outskirts of the city.

Through busy shopping streets,
	past squares and fountains,
	right up to the doorstep
		of Adin's building.

"Mama, come and see!" shouted Adin.
"Well, would you look at that," she said,
	smiling as she saw the blanket of blossom below.
"It's a trail," said Adin. "And it leads from here to…"

But Adin's mother knew exactly where it led.
She picked up the keys to their new car,
	and said, "A trail is meant to be followed…
		don't you think?"

Lanterns glowed in the cherry trees that evening.
Adin and Dina sat
    back to back
    beneath a cherry-blossom sky.

And that is where they stayed all evening,
    together,
    like twin cherries
        on the same stem.